AARON SLATER, ILLUSTRATOR

To David
—A.B.

For all my fellow illustrators
who tell stories with their art
—D.R.

The illustrations in this book were made with watercolors,
pen, and ink on Arches paper.

Cataloging-in-Publication Data has been applied for and may be
obtained from the Library of Congress.

ISBN 978-1-4197-5396-1
Text copyright © 2021 Andrea Beaty
Illustrations copyright © 2021 David Roberts
Book design by Heather Kelly

Published in 2021 by Abrams Books for Young Readers,
an imprint of ABRAMS. All rights reserved. No portion of this book may
be reproduced, stored in a retrieval system, or transmitted in any form or
by any means, mechanical, electronic, photocopying, recording,
or otherwise, without written permission from the publisher.

Printed and bound in U.S.A.

10 9 8 7 6 5 4 3 2 1

Abrams Books for Young Readers are available at special discounts when
purchased in quantity for premiums and promotions as well as fundraising
or educational use. Special editions can also be created to specification.
For details, contact specialsales@abramsbooks.com or the address below.

Abrams® is a registered trademark of Harry N. Abrams, Inc.

ABRAMS The Art of Books
195 Broadway, New York, NY 10007
abramsbooks.com

AARON SLATER, ILLUSTRATOR

by **Andrea Beaty**
illustrated by **David Roberts**
Abrams Books for Young Readers, New York

At the end of the garden, in the soft, fading light,

when the day turns to dusk and the dusk into night,

the sweet scent of jasmine floats into the air

to mix with the music of laughter, and there . . .

Aaron D. Slater soaks it all in

with his flowery blanket tucked under his chin.

Words drift like music. Melodious. Mild.

A sweet summer song for a sweet summer child

who drifts off to sleep as the cottonwoods sway

at the end of the garden. At the end of the day.

It's summer, then summer, and summer once more,
and soon Aaron D. is a youngster of four.
The jasmine climbs higher. The roses have grown.
And Aaron himself has a spot of his own
for seedlings and saplings beside the slate walk,
which he illustrates daily with a bucket of chalk.

But what he loves most—what makes Aaron's heart sing—
is to listen to books in the old garden swing.
To write stories, he thinks, *is the greatest of things.*

But first, he must read. It's the best place to start,

and young Aaron wants to with all of his heart.

But the words are just squiggles, and try though he might,

AARON TRIES AGAIN WITH NEVE, WITH HELP HE THOUGHT HE'D GET IT RIGHT

even with help Aaron can't get it right.

"Why can't I do it? Why is it so hard?"

He goes back to drawing on slate in his yard.

It's schooltime at last!

In his sunflower socks

and poppy-red jacket and with matching lunchbox,

he marches to class with a teacher's bouquet

ready to read by the end of the day.

But he doesn't that day—or that month or that year—

and though he makes progress, it's painfully clear

he'll never quite get it like all of his friends.

Since he'll never stand out, he decides to blend in.

And so here he is at the start of Grade Two

in his simple white T-shirt and matching white shoes.

He tries to keep up. To blend in. And to hide

the tangle of feelings he carries inside.

At first, it goes well, since his teacher is new

and a bit overwhelmed by the hullabaloo,

but things settle down and Miss Greer finds her stride,

and once she gets rolling, there's no place to hide.

"Class," she says, "here's an assignment for you.

Write me a story. Write something true."

And so Aaron does what young Aaron must do.

He works on his story like the rest of Grade Two.

He writes through the evening.

He writes through the night.

He writes and he writes

till the dawn's early light.

Then he drags off to school with his shoes filled with lead

and his stomach in knots and a pain in his head,

and he waits for his turn with his heart filled with dread.

Miss Greer calls his name, and Aaron D. stands

and unfolds the sheet in his trembling hands.

And he reads . . . well, he tries . . .

but it's so hard to start

with thirty-three eyes peering into his heart.

So he stares at his shoes and his sunflower socks,

then he closes his eyes,

and then young Aaron talks.

"ONCE . . . well . . . once . . . there was . . . a flower . . .

No . . . wait . . . I know . . .

Once there was *a magical* flower . . .

which gave all who held it *extraordinary* power!"

And so begins the most perfect of tales

of an imperfect hero whose courage fails

when the day turns to dusk and the dusk into night

and the moon rises high and the dragons take flight.

And who learns after all, in the wee morning hours:

Strength comes from the heart and not magical flowers.

That beauty and kindness and loving and art

lend courage to all with a welcoming heart.

And when the quest ends and the sweet flower dies,

the students all gasp and Miss Lila Greer cries.

The silence that follows rattles his heart.

He tries to say something, but where could he start?

He turns in a paper with no words at all,

then blinks back a tear and escapes to the hall

where Miss Lila finds him by the slate-colored wall.

Time stops for them both, the teacher and boy.

His heart fills with anguish.

And hers?

Hers fills with joy at the soul of this artist,

courageous and true.

She smiles and whispers, "Aaron . . .

Thank you."

When she leaves, Aaron stands there a very long while

then slowly . . . so slowly . . . he begins to smile,

and he feels like he does with those books in the swing.

As a new hope inside starts to make his heart sing,

he knows he can do the greatest of things

in a way that's his own—in a way that's just his—

he can stand out and show the whole world who *he* is.

Like the mightiest flames that banish the dark,

hope grows in the soul from the tiniest spark.

His art makes the difference. His art leads the way

and helps him discover what he wants to say.

And his reading gets better. Of course, it's still tough,

but each day that they work is a little less rough.

Like all imperfect heroes at the start of a quest,

he must do what he can and hope for the best.

Now, in the hallway, a new garden grows

with jasmine and poppies. A rambling rose.

Books. Art and music. A dragon or two

who soar through a sky of delphinium blue.

The art tells a story: Melodious. Mild.

Furious. Fragrant. Wonderful. Wild.

It's all from the heart. And all of it's true.

For Aaron, Miss Greer, and the kids of Grade Two,

it's a place full of beauty, for one and for all:

the Illustrator's Garden at the end of the hall.

A NOTE ON THE TYPE

This text has been set in Dyslexie, a typeface specially designed for people with dyslexia. To learn more, visit Dyslexiefont.com.

AUTHOR'S NOTE

Aaron Douglas Slater is named after Aaron Douglas, an African American painter, muralist, and graphic artist who lived from 1899 to 1979. He was a key figure in the Harlem Renaissance, an important literary and artistic movement of the 1920s and '30s. Douglas's art was influenced by African art, Art Deco, and jazz and reflected African American life and struggles. Jazz instruments, such as trombones and trumpets, appear in many of his works.

Learning to read is hard for Aaron Slater. His brain has difficulty identifying how speech sounds relate to letters and words. Aaron has dyslexia, just like fifteen to twenty percent of all people. There are many other learning difficulties people may have. For instance, dysgraphia is difficulty learning to write. Dyscalculia is a form of difficulty doing math. Some people have difficulty focusing, which is called attention deficit disorder (ADD) or attention deficit hyperactivity disorder (ADHD).

These learning problems are not about a person's intelligence, creativity, kindness, willingness to work, or their awesomeness. They are just about how the person's brain works. All of these difficulties (and many others) can be frustrating, but tools and special instruction from educators and others can help.

Aaron's dyslexia informs who he is, but it does not define who he is. We each have our own superpowers and struggles. That's what makes us unique, beautiful, strong, and important to the world. Just like Aaron.

ILLUSTRATOR'S NOTE

As someone who struggled with reading and spelling (and still does), I quickly learned how to read and tell stories with pictures! A picture can play with our imagination, make us feel the heat of the glowing sun on a cold winter's day, or feel the wind billowing through leaves when all is quiet and still. We can share in someone's sadness or their joy through pictures. Telling stories with Aaron through drawings has made this a very special book for me. I hope you enjoy it.